E.L. Moran

An "Elizabeth" story

By: Shaquan McDowell

This book was published as an extension of the "Elizabeth" project.

Introduction & Foreword

Ever since I was a kid, I have had this deep thirst and love for all things history: The stories of those who came before inspired me and continue to today. More often than not, however, I couldn't find people who looked like me, within the history textbooks. Throughout time, I learned to find those stories on my own, to connect with people like me that came before. E.L.Moran is a series that seeks to do the same: to help students who fail to see themselves in the historical narrative, come to understand the role that people like themselves played. I hope that children, like my own nieces and nephews, will be able to envision themselves in the grander story of history, in a way that they have been deprived of before.

I dedicate this book to my nieces and nephews: Mya, Jaziah, Jhari, Sasha, and Mckenzie, and my maternal grandmother Shirley Mae, whose family serves as inspiration for this story.
-   S.C. MCD

Table of Contents:

Chapter 1: My Name is Elizabeth

My name is Elizabeth L. Moran. The L stands for something, but I don't really know what it means. I do know my name very well though. It's probably because mom says it a lot, and sometimes in a really serious way. It's usually on Monday mornings when I don't want to get out of bed. But hey, who wants to get out of bed on a Monday? My Mom takes me to school every morning. I enjoy the car ride.

On Mondays, we grab breakfast along the way, at my favorite restaurant. Mom always orders a coffee: four creamers, and 2 scoops of sugar, a small dash of cinnamon, and finished with whipped cream on top. We then turn on the radio and listen to mom's playlist. I usually don't know most of the songs, but I just dance along anyway. And then I usually spill something accidentally

That's when mom turns to me and goes, "Elizabeth L. Moran, how many times have I told you to properly hold your food in the car?"

Until one day I finally asked her, "Mom why do you do that?"

"What?"

"Why is it whenever I do something wrong, you go "Elizabeth L. Moran" and wave your finger in the air? I'm not the finger patrol, but I'm sure that finger has more serious business to take care of"

Mom must've liked my joke, because she did laugh a little, before answering my question.

"Because your name is important and has power. It's who you are, and special. It is how people will always remember you."

"So why did you name me Elizabeth? There are a million other people named Elizabeth. And the L? We could all do without the L."

"Your name is really special Elizabeth. It's the name of one of your ancestors. One of my ancestors too."

"Well, who are they? I think I should know, especially if I'm going to be named after them."

"I'll be more than happy to tell you all about who they were, right after you get out of school."

I didn't even notice the school outside when mom's car stopped. If I had my way, we would've kept talking then and there. I am a kid though, and kids must respect their parents. So, I choose the smartest choice: to listen.

It didn't mean I didn't think about it, though. I did. Throughout the day. Especially during social studies. My teacher, Ms. Allison was teaching us about

American History and all about the 13 colonies. I wondered where my ancestors fit into it all, and I couldn't wait for mom to tell me. I could imagine my ancestor, holding a musket, standing on the front lines; a patriot to their core.

When class finally came to the end for the day, Ms. Allison told me goodbye. I did the same, and told her that I'd be ready for any quiz about social studies the next day. I mean, my ancestors practically lived it: How could I fail?

When I got outside, mom was already there waiting for me. I could tell she had been there for a while. There was a bit of bird poop on her right window, from the tree in the parking lot, but she wasn't under it anymore. So, I could tell she had moved up overtime.

You see Mom is never late, and that's probably why she wants me awake on-time on Monday. I take my time coming out of the school, from time to time. Mom never minds though. She always is there waiting, when I finally come out the double doors.

That day though, I got into the car, and got straight to the point.

"Alright, so tell me more".

"Wow. What a smile and such excitement. I guess someone had a great day at school.", Mom said with a smile.

"Well, yes actually. It's going to get even better though, when you tell me how big my ancestor Elizabeth was in the American Revolution."

Mom's smile turned into a curious face.

"So, are you going to tell me."

"Not now, I have a few errands to run. I'll tell you before bed."

"But you promised.", I wasn't taking no for an answer. I had waited all day for the story

"I promise we can have pizza for dinner, if you will go on these errands with me."

Then and there, I had a change of heart. I had waited all day. What's the harm in waiting a little longer? The errands took about 3 hours to finish, and we got home around 6:30. Mom kept her promise and before we got to the house, we stopped at our favorite Pizza place *A.J. 's Pizza*, and picked up a large Ham & Pineapple. Mom says never to call it Hawaiian Pizza, because it came from Canada not Hawaii, and that name is just wrong.

I rushed into the house and washed my hands, and got straight to work on the pizza. I must've eaten so much that it hypnotized me, because before I knew it 2 hours had gone by and I was already in bed.

"So now, will you tell me about Elizabeth?" I asked. Mom brushed my hair back and smiled, as she looked at me.

"Sure, my love, but I don't think she's exactly what you're expecting."

I was still a bit hazy and hypnotized by the Pizza as I asked, "Is she completely amazing and cool?"

She smiled a bit and kissed my forehead. She leaned into my ear and said "Cooler than you will ever know?"

"Then, she's exactly what I'm expecting."

I could see mom's grin grow bigger, as she began to tell the story. I closed my eyes and just listened.

"Elizabeth was born in 1810, in a small town in South Carolina. This is a time where many white people thought that black people should be slaves. The people who did this were not good at all. Elizabeth's family was a little different though, she was born free."

I don't remember much else that mom said after that. The pizza managed to knock me out so fast, and I drifted further and further into sleep.

And then I woke up.

.

Chapter 2: Welcome to Walnut Grove

When I woke up, I wasn't in my bed anymore. I thought that was a little weird, but Mom says I'm known for my sleepwalking. Usually, I just end up on the couch, but I'd been doing so well in P.E., I probably would have walked miles before mom knew. Luckily, it was daylight out, even if I didn't know what time. That meant I had a good night's sleep, and I'd be good to go. I started walking for a little while.

The air smelled clear and there didn't seem to be any clouds in the sky. There were no cars. No skyscrapers. No buses. No lights. No roads. No stop signs (which is really bad, because I love stop signs). There was nothing but grass, trees, and fields for miles and miles. Except, next to one of the trees was a little girl. She looked like she was my age, so I decided to walk over to her and say hello. That's when she grabbed something off of the tree and put it right in her nose.

I didn't mean to be rude, but I couldn't help but say, "Eww.", as she put it up to her nose and inhaled.

"I don't mean to interrupt, but that's unsanitary."

I must have scared her pretty bad because she immediately ran around a corner.

"Geez, I'm so sorry. I didn't mean to scare you."

She peeped at me from around the trunk of a tree.

"What's unsanitary?", she whispered.

"Not clean. Dirty. Not what you want to pull up to your face".

She smiled a little bit and laughed, before putting the thing in her hand right up to my nose.

"This ain't unsanitary. It's a magnolia. The kinda thing you want to put on your face and nose. Here.", she said as she stuffed the puffy white flower in front of my face.

I have to admit, it smelled pretty good.

"Ok. You're right. That's pretty delicious. I've never heard of magnolia before. Not even in school"

"You go to school?", she asked.

"Of course, I go to school. All kids go to school. It's the law."

"Around here it ain't the law. Most kids don't go to school unless you're rich."

"Well, I must not be from around here then, because where I am from, we all go to school, even when we don't feel like it".

"Don't feel like it? Who wouldn't want to go to school and learn?"

As I looked at her face and saw how confused she was, it started to set in on me that I wasn't back home anymore.

"Ok, enough with the questions. Can you tell me

where I am?", I asked.

I didn't want to cut her off, but this was an emergency.

"This is Walnut Grove"

"What's a Walnut Grove? I've never been to a Walnut Grove a day in my life. I've only been to an apple farm a few times in the fall".

That made her laugh pretty hard, and when she explained to me that Walnut Grove was a place in South Carolina and not a farm where they produced walnuts, I understood how funny it must have been.

"South Carolina? I know I've been doing great in P.E., but there's no way I walked from Virginia to South Carolina, in one night".

As I paced back and forth, the girl stared at me while pulling on one of her curls, until she finally spoke

"Can I ask you a question this time, since you've asked me some and asked yourself quite a few already?",

She had a point there, so I couldn't say no.,

"Go ahead, but you gotta make it quick. I'm dealing with an emergency here."

I didn't know what kind of question she would ask, so I was a little nervous.

"What's your name?", she asked quickly.

That was a question I certainly knew the answer to.

"Elizabeth L. Moran at your service. Shortest in my class, but got lots of smarts and sass."

"Oh, that's great. My name is Elizabeth too. But everyone calls me Betsy", she said excitedly.

"I'll call you Betsy then, just not to get confused. What is with everyone and the name Elizabeth? You would think people would be a little more creative in the 21st century."

"What's the 21st century?", she asked.

"You know, like the year we live in", I explained.

"Oh, 1819?", she asked.

"1819?", I thought to myself. "South Carolina is pretty far, but I'm sure 1819 is further".

Before I had a chance to ask her anything else, I turned around and saw her running away across the field.

"Hey, where are you going?", I screamed.

"I have to get back home to pick the greens for dinner, or Mama will be upset. You can come if you want."

Though I didn't know what it meant to pick greens for dinner, what I did know is that moms were good at fixing issues, and I hoped her mom could do that for me too. So, I tagged along. It took me a while to catch up with her. I'm sure she'd do much better than me in P.E.

Sweating and tired I asked her, "Why aren't you tired?".

"Tired? This is easy.", she said.

Maybe for her, it was, but for me, it was too much. Too tired to move, my body forced me to the ground. My legs were on fire. Betsy didn't skip a beat though.

"Aren't you going to take a break", I suggested.

"I got to pick the greens for dinner, or Mama won't be able to make them tonight.", she said as she bent down and started picking a little leaf ball growing from the ground.

When I managed to lift up and look further, I noticed quite a few green leaf balls growing from the ground.

"What are you picking?", I asked

"The Greens. Haven't you had collard greens before?"

My grandad had made something called greens a few times before. I thought about those and said, "They weren't very good".

"Well after you eat these, you'll never say nothing like that again for sure. Mama makes the best greens I ever had. But first, we gotta pick 'em.", she said with a smile.

"Can you show me how?", I asked.

Other than a flower once in kindergarten for my mom, I had never picked anything a day in my life, especially not food. Betsy kept picking stuff though, so: If I couldn't beat her, I would join her. Plus, if the food was as good as she said, the faster we got it done, the faster we could eat. The pizza from the night before was starting to wear off.

"Sure. Just take your hand, put it on the leaf, and push down", and it immediately snapped right off.

"Wow, that's easy."

"I'm glad you think so because we got a lot more to do."

She immediately put me straight to work, but I didn't mind. The faster I got food in my stomach, the happier I would be. I got to ask Betsy a few more questions as we worked too.

"Betsy, do you have to pick all your food?"

"No. Some of it we grow, some of it we raise, and some of it we buy in-town at the general. Mama doesn't like to go in-town too much though".

"Why not?", I asked her.

"Well, because of slavery", she said, "She wants to keep me and her safe".

I had heard about slavery in social studies, but my

teacher didn't say much. I knew that a long time ago, in a year like 1810, many people in America thought it was ok to keep others as people. Black people were made to do all the work for White people, and White people got all the credit and Black people were hurt if they didn't do what the white person said.

"Are you and your mom slaves?", I asked quietly.

"No, we're not.", she said,

"But my family used to be. We used to live in Virginia but moved down this way before I was born. My family got their freedom there."

Hearing Virginia made me excited.

"I'm from Virginia.", I said.

"Are you a slave?", she asked me.

"No. Where I'm from, there is no slavery".

"Oh, you must be from far up north then", she said surely.

That was true, but not exactly what I meant. I could say anything though, before Betsy grabbed all the collards are started toward a small wood cabin, next to the field. I followed her Once inside, she grabbed a pot and put the greens inside. She grabbed some water, poured it into the pot , and started cleaning them.

"There, all done. Mama will be happy for sure.", she said as she finally breathed a sigh of relief.

"You sure do talk about your Mama a lot, she must be something special".

"More than special. My Mama is the smartest and best person I know.".

Seeing the way Betsy's eyes glowed when she talked about her mom, made me think about my mom too, and how she wouldn't cook dinner unless the kitchen was a certain way. She'd spend what seemed like forever refolding the clothes on the kitchen stove, or messing cleaning the counters over and over again.

"Mama's save us kids", I said jokingly.

"Not just kids. Mama's save us all", she replied.

As soon as we started talking about moms, Betsy's mom strolled in. She was sweating just a little, as she carried a heavy bag over her shoulder. With her hair tied into a ponytail and her dress dragging across the floor, the sweat didn't matter at all, cause I could see exactly what Betsy had meant; She reminded me of my mama so much.

"Betsy, did you do what I ask and pick the greens?", Betsy's mom asked.

"Yes, Mama. They're right here."

"Thank you, baby. ", she said as she kissed Betsy's forehead and rubbed her face.

"I brought some pork down at the general store. We'll throw it in there and make us something nice."

That's when she finally noticed me.

"And who might you be", she asked staring straight at me. I must've taken a while to respond cause she followed up with, "Don't be shy. You've got nothing to worry about here."

"Elizabeth", I said softly

"Speak up now child. Be confident when you say your name. It's who you are. ", she said sternly.

"Elizabeth L. Moran", I replied strongly.

She chuckled a little.

"I can see your mama has quite the mind.", she said.

"Elizabeth says she a lot like you", Betsy added

Betsy's mom's smile grew a little wider: All of her teeth were showing.

"I'm sure that is such an honor", her mom replied.

"You can call me Miss Scott", she said to me.

I was just glad to hear I wouldn't have to think of another name for Elizabeth.

"Now, I'm sure you both are quite hungry. I know I am. Let's get these greens done so that we all can eat.", Miss Scott said before she started cooking.

Having Miss Scott there made me feel more at ease. The day had been completely crazy, and I couldn't wait to get back home, but Miss Scott made me feel safer.

Chapter 3: Miss Scott's Secret

After we finished eating, I noticed outside that the sky had started to turn a light purple. I could tell the sun had begun to set, and that it would be nighttime soon. I thought about Mama and my bed, but most important my bed (just kidding, Mama is most important). Miss Scott saw me staring.

"Don't worry Elizabeth, we will get you home", she said.

"I know. It's just a long way to go", I replied.

I was sure I could walk to Virginia if I ever needed to, but time traveling was something I hadn't figured out yet (or so I thought?).

"You aren't from around, here are you?"

"How'd you know?", I asked.

She pulled on my pajama pants. I forgot I had been wearing those all day.

"Most girls don't dress in these kinds of clothes around here", Miss Scott joked with a grin across her face.

All-day I had been trying to act like I belonged when my clothes had been a dead giveaway, the entire time.

"Where are you from?", She asked me

I wanted to tell her the truth and tell her I had been zapped back in time, but I thought she wouldn't believe me.

"Virginia.", I responded.

Miss Scott looked at me for a while, squinting both of her eyes. I could tell that she knew I was leaving something out. I didn't say anything else though."

"You know, my folks are from Virginia. Some of them still live there too.", she told me.

"Betsy told me, ma'am", I answered.

"Did she now?", she said as she grabbed Betsy's knee and shook it proudly.

"Yes, she did", I once again replied, "She also told me about…", I got silent. I had a question and I knew I wanted to ask it, but I didn't know how.

"Go ahead now. Speak your mind", Miss Scott reassured me.

"Slavery. She told me about slavery", I said.

"That's all?", Miss Scott asked.

It didn't seem shocking to her at all. For me though, it was very shocking. I had heard about it in Social Studies class before, but not a lot about it. It was often in between the stuff we talked about more like the American Revolution, the Civil War, or even the War of 1812.

"Yes. We don't have slavery where I come from.", I explained.

After I said that, it seemed to all make sense to Miss Scott and Betsy. They both looked at me with caring eyes, as Betsy came over and sat next to me.

"Slavery is a very bad thing Elizabeth. Some very bad people who treat others wrongly, because of the way they look. They don't treat them like people at all.", Miss Scott continued, "But we must always remember that everyone in those chains is a human being, with their own story, their own family, and their own lives. We can't forget that. That's our job, cause they're our people."

"But you're not a slave, and neither is Betsy.", I said.

"Yes, but a long time ago in Virginia my family were slaves. One of my grandmothers long ago was free, and so now Betsy and I are free today. We are linked to everyone on every plantation. Their stories are our stories", she told me.

I had never heard that before or heard of anyone talk about people who were enslaved that way. Other than a paragraph in my history textbook, I had never much about them at all. It made me want to know more, and learn more about others who may have been enslaved, even people from my own family.

I decided to ask Betsy and Miss Scott about their family's history and where they came from. They told me about how at the start of America the first slaves were brought on ships to the country. They also told me and that many people of color who were free, were the children, of those first slaves. I couldn't believe that had happened and been left out of history books. It even happened in my home state, Virginia, and I had no clue.

"What about the Revolution? Did you have any family on the battleground and apart of the action?"

"Everybody with family from Virginia knew somebody in the War. The story goes that it was a free black man named Crispus Attucks, who first gave his life for the country", Miss Scott told me, "There were plenty more who supported the effort and those in front of it all. Ole' Willie Lee with General George and Little Miss Sally with Thomas Jefferson, to name a few, but there were many more.

It was shocking to hear so many names that I

was used to when talking about history, paired with so many I had never heard about. I wanted to keep talking and learn as much as I can, but I slowly saw the oil in the lamp started to go out. When I looked outside, it was no longer purple. The colors of the sunset were replaced with a dark sky, with little sparkles of light throughout. I had never seen the sky so pretty; it almost looked alive.

"The oil is out, light is gone. Time to get both of you in bed."

There was only one bed in the house, so I knew Betsy and I would have to share.

"Here, this should fit you fine", Betsy handed me a gown, which was just a little smaller than her own.

I threw the gown over my pajamas and crawled into bed, as Miss Scott came over to tuck us in. She tossed a blanket over the both of us, rubbed our hair with her hands, and began to say a prayer over both of us. She then walked back across the room and sat in a chair looking out the window.

I tried to close my eyes and sleep, but I couldn't help but think about getting home. I laid in bed for a few minutes, before turning over to check on Betsy. She was completely asleep. I shut my eyes again and closed tighter until I realized it was a lost cause. Miss Scott was still awake and sitting in the chair next to the door. I slipped out of bed and tried to slip into the chair next to her. She noticed me as I moved across the room.

"Well, look who is up and about", she said softly.

"Sorry. I just couldn't sleep.", I explained to her.

I didn't want her thinking I was a kid who didn't follow the rules, because I do follow the rules.

"Not a worry, child. Come, sit with me."

I sat right next to her, as she looked out into the night, out the window next to the door.

"Aren't you going to go to sleep", I asked her

"In a little while. I like to stay up a little later and keep watch over my Betsy", she said to me.

"Are you afraid?", I asked.

She got quiet and looked at me. She stared, then she smiled some more.

"No, because I have my Betsy, I have good friends and family, I have hope, and I have faith", she replied to me.

"In what?", I asked.

"That things will get better. That God will make them better. I'll even let you in on a little secret.", she teased.

"What is it?", I asked her

I loved to hear secrets, and I was well known for keeping my lips sealed (unless it was too good, of course).

She promised she'd tell me, but only if I'd agree to get back in bed and try to go to sleep. I started to get the idea that parents liked to make really good deals, so I agreed to hers, and walked back over to the bed and hopped in. As promised she kneeled next to my ear, whispered a secret into it. It was a wonderful secret. I asked her if I could share it with others and she said yes. I smiled and fell asleep.

Chapter 4: Hello, Hampton

As I opened my eyes the next morning, the first thing I noticed was my memory foam mattress beneath my back. It was the best feeling I had ever felt, as I realized I was back home. Even better, I realized that for the first time, I was up earlier than mom was.

I ran toward her room screaming "Mom, we're going to be late.". I knew this would be the only chance I had to flip the roles once. I had to take it.

"For someone who fell asleep after stuffing themselves with pizza, I'm surprised to see that you have so much energy", she said wearily.
"Yea, that's what picking greens will do for you."

I could tell by the confused look on Mom's face, that she didn't understand what that meant at all.

"I need you to wake up. I have to get to school, and you still owe the rest of the story about my name", I insisted.

"Tell you what, you give me 5 more minutes of sleeping and I will be up and ready and happily tell you everything you want to know", she bargained.

"Deal, but no more deals. I'm starting to feel like I'm the one losing in these agreements", I insisted.

Mom kept her promise, and we were up and out the door in no time. Though it wasn't Monday, mom said that we could stop for breakfast. Mom was shocked when I asked the cook if collard greens were on the menu for dinner and then told him they should be, if they were not. He agreed with that, and so I took that as progress. As we drove along the road, singing to mom's playlist, I noticed us take a new turn.

"Where are we going", I asked

"I promised you the rest of the story. I keep my promises."

We drove for a little while, before coming across a sign that said *Entering Hampton, VA*. I could see the water's edge get closer, as we drove along. After crossing a few bridges and getting close enough to the water that we could jump right in. Then, mom stopped the car.

"Where are we?", I asked her

"In a way, we are home", she replied before adding, "In 1619, some of the first African slaves in America were brought here, to this very spot. Back then, it was called *Port Comfort, VA*. Slavery was a very bad time in our history, but our family survived, and we today come from the people brought here long ago".

This made me think about what Miss Scott had told me about every slave on every plantation and how their stories were our stories too.

Mom then pulled out a silver charm bracelet, with one tiny round charm on hand on its end. She placed it right in my hand. As I looked at it hard, I could tell that it was a Walnut.

"What's this for?", I asked her, "Sorry for all the

questions today, I guess it's my new thing."

"I love your questions. Ask as many as you like. ", she assured me before answering, "Some of our family who came from here, were set free, and lived in South Carolina, in a small town called Walnut Grove.", she answered.

Walnut Grove was where Miss Scott and Betsy lived. I started to wonder if maybe they had met my family and wondered if they had lived next door.

"One of them was named Elizabeth Scott. She was born in 1810, but everyone called her Betsy. You are named after her", she continued.

As mom kept talking I held the charm bracelet in my hand and stared at it. I couldn't help but put the pieces together: not only did Betsy and I have the same name, but I think I had stolen hers. No matter what I was proud, and I couldn't help but smile from ear to ear.

"Why are you smiling so hard", mom asked.

"Because, I have an extra special treat for Social Studies class today", I explained.

From the look on mom's face, I sensed a little bit of fear and curiosity.

"You have nothing to worry about mom. I'm just going to help tell the full story like you told me", I assured her.

Chapter 5: Setting it Straight in Social Studies

We pulled up to my school about 20 minutes after leaving Hampton. I excitedly opened the door and tried to rush outside. Before I could get away though, Mama grabbed my backpack.

"Elizabeth, remember to behave", she said with a slight smirk across her lips.

"I promised. I just can't wait for social studies today", I said before hopping out of the car, heading toward the school.

I couldn't wait to share all I had learned with my classmates. There was so much about History and Social Studies that we had never known, and I was to be the teacher and tell everyone.

I had to wait a while though. Social studies weren't covered until the end of the day, but I made sure to let my teacher Mrs. Allison knew that I had something important to share. After we came back in from recess, it was finally time for Social Studies. I knew the topic of the day was the Civil War. I had heard about this before and heard my teachers in second grade go on and on about Abraham Lincoln, U.S. Grant, Sherman, and Lee. I knew it was about much more than that though

As Miss Allison began the lesson, I waved her down from my desk.

"Wait", I said, "Oh, yes, Elizabeth. I almost forgot. Please go ahead", Miss Allison said as she gave me the floor.

Walking to the front of the classroom, I looked at the charm bracelet that mom had given me. I twisted my wrist to feel it move, as I remembered me and mama's trip, smelling magnolia with Betsy, and the words of Miss Scott had told me. As I turned to the rest of the class, I took a deep breath in and let the words flow out.

"I'm sure we've all heard about the Civil War and how it was fought because of slavery, but do you know the stories of those who were enslaved? They matter too, and while it's important to learn about people like General Lee and President Lincoln, it is also important that we learn the stories of the people this mattered to most. Also, many people think that the Civil War was the first-time people fought for the freedom of black people. That's not true. The first American Patriot was a black man, Crispus Attucks. Some people of color were even free back in the 1600s, even right here in Virginia."

As I finished my sentence, I looked around the classroom. I had all my classmates' attention. Walking back to my seat I could hear them whisper, "Great job" and "I want to know more", and all I could keep thinking to myself was, "You won't learn that in social studies class every day".

It felt so great to be able to teach my classmates something new about history.

Chapter 6: The History Book

As always, after school mama was on time. In fact, she was more than on time. I could see the bird poop on the windshield, from the tree in the parking lot. I knew once I stepped in the car, mom would want to know all about how my day had gone.

"It was great", I answered her

"Just great, I know that there's more to the story than just great", she teased.

She was right though. It was more than great. Everyone loved what I had to say and wanted to know even more. Ms. Allison had given me a special notebook and told me that I should write down other stories I heard or learned about. It made me feel like a detective. Mom saw the notebook, and asked if she could see it. I said she could.

"Wow, this is nice. What is it?", she asked.

"It's my history book", I answered.

"History books look a lot different than they looked when I was growing up", she joked.

"No mom, not that kind of history book. It's a book where I can write down all the stories I learn that might not be in our regular history book. Ms. Allison gave it to me, and told me to share any stories that I want.", I explained.

Mom smiled a little. I could tell that it made her happy to hear that I was loving history. She asked me more about the day as we drove home, and I told her all about how I wanted to learn more. She promised to take me to the library and the archives (whatever that is?), to learn as much as I wanted. When we got home, I took my journal and ran straight up to my room.

"You don't want any of the leftover pizza?", she asked.

"No thanks mom, I've got some writing to do", I told her, "Although if you make some collard greens, let me know", I insisted.

She laughed a little and waved me up the stairs.

I got to my room, laid the journal on my desk, and started to write. There was one more thing I needed to add and tell, and who better to tell, than my history book. As I opened it and began to write on the first page, I thought about Miss Scott's Secret. And then I wrote:

*My name is Elizabeth L. Moran. I was named after one of my many great grandmothers, named Elizabeth. She was born in Walnut Grove, SC and was a free person of color. The name Elizabeth is special because it has hope. It means **God is My Abundance** and reminds us that even when times seem hard, God always has our back. That's why her mom gave it to her, and why my mom gave it to me.*

As I finished writing, I could see mom leaning over my shoulder and holding a plate of pizza. She was smiling as she read what I wrote.

"Mom", I shouted, "No peeking."

"Ok!", she agreed, "I just thought that you might get a little hungry."

She sat the pizza on my desk and began to walk away.

"Wait, I have more questions", I said.

"Go ahead.", she said.

"What about the L? What's the L for?", I asked her.

She laughed and shook her head, before saying "That's a story for another day".

I agreed with her. I could wait for the story to happen on another day. Little did mom know though, I would make sure that the day would be tomorrow.

More About the Author

    Shaquan McDowell is a Brandeis University graduate and academic in Early American History and American politics. As a part of his concentration, he studies community building and the evolution of Free People of Color communities, and their impact on contemporary communal relations.

    Shaquan enjoys helping others learn who they are, through connecting them with their heritage genealogically. He believes that understanding the lives of those who came before, can help us navigate our uncharted territories. He is the host of the "Genealogical Gentleman" podcast on Spotify and has worked in UK Parliament and MTV News as an active contributor.

Made in the USA
Coppell, TX
05 February 2021